# The Grasshopper
## and the Butterfly

Joe Swartz
Illustrated by Ansley McLeod

Published by Orange Hat Publishing 2021
ISBN 9781645382997

Copyright © 2021 by Joe Swartz
The Grasshopper and the Butterfly
Written by Joe Swartz
Illustrated by Ansley McLeod

All Rights Reserved. Written permission must be secured from the publisher to use or reproduce any part of this book, except for brief quotations in critical reviews or articles.

For information, please contact:

Orange Hat Publishing
www.orangehatpublishing.com
Waukesha, WI

For my daughter Sophie. Try new things, take chances, and grow into the best version of yourself you can be. I love you so much!
*–Joe*

---

To my grandfather, whose beautiful woodworking inspired the butterfly and bird houses within these pages. To the residents of Madison, Wisconsin's east side, whose gardens inspired the plethora of flowers and wildlife within this book.
*–Ansley*

Once upon a time, in the town of Backlawnsville, there were two tiny eggs.

The two eggs had been laid very close together and talked to keep each other company.

"Hello, neighbor. I am a butterfly egg. What are you?" asked the one egg to the other.

"I am a grasshopper egg," the other egg replied.

"Do you want to be my friend?" asked the butterfly egg.

"That would be great. I cannot wait until we hatch, so we can run and play like friends do!" exclaimed the grasshopper egg.

Days passed and the eggs began to hatch…

Out of the butterfly egg emerged a small larva.

Out of the grasshopper egg emerged a small nymph.

"You tricked me!" yelled the grasshopper nymph. "You told me you were a butterfly egg, and you look nothing like a butterfly! I cannot be friends with someone who does not tell the truth."

"I am not a liar," explained the butterfly larva. "I will be a butterfly, you will see. As I grow, I go through a process called complete metamorphosis, where I look different in each of the four stages of my life cycle. In this second stage, I am a caterpillar, which is another name for butterfly larva."

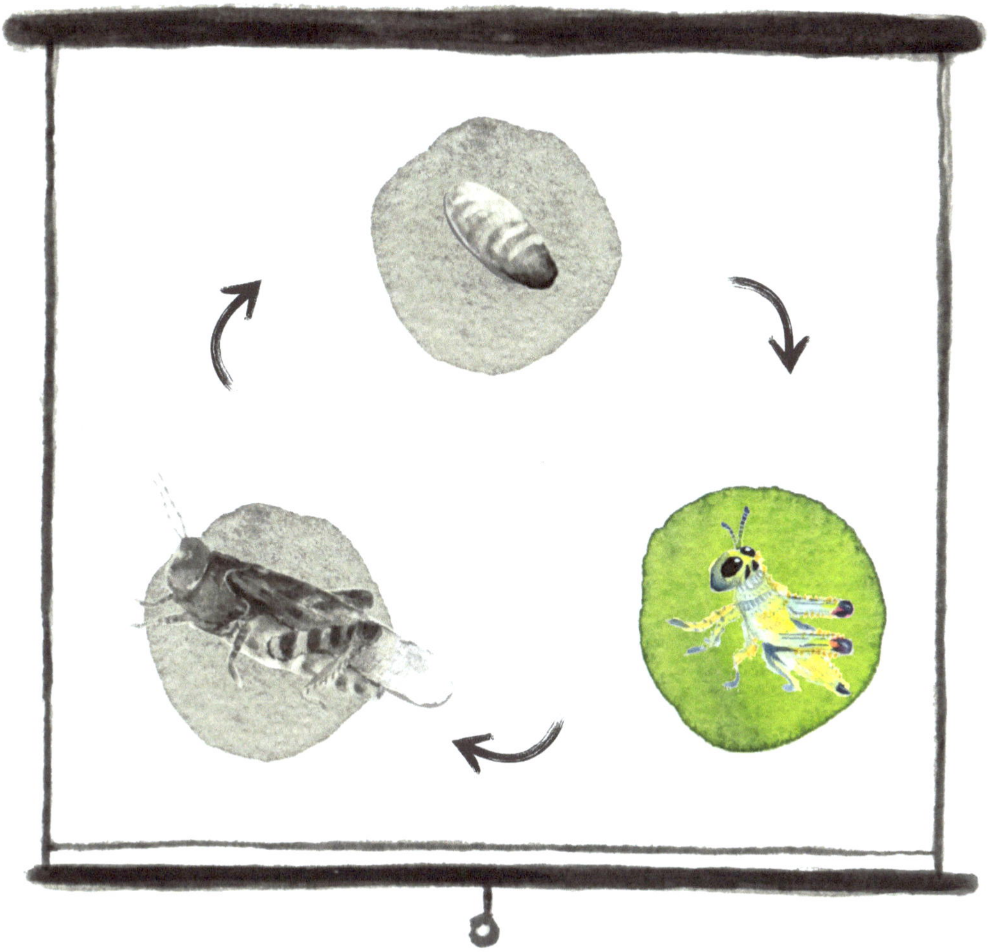

The grasshopper nymph replied, "Thank you for explaining that to me so we can still be friends. I go through metamorphosis as I grow too, but it is called incomplete metamorphosis. I only have three stages in my life cycle, and I will look similar in my final stage to how I look now. I am currently in the nymph stage."

The caterpillar and the grasshopper nymph continued to grow and enjoyed life outside of their eggs.

They played together and ate leaves until one day...
The caterpillar said, "I am full. I am going to go on that branch and rest a little bit."

The caterpillar climbed up to a nice spot and then made a silk pad on the underside of the branch. The caterpillar then hung upside down from the pad.

"What are you doing?" asked the grasshopper nymph.

"I am making a chrysalis to sleep in," the caterpillar said. "It will help keep me safe and warm. I think I am going to stay here for a while. This is the third stage of my life cycle, the last one before I become a butterfly. I am now in my pupa stage."

The grasshopper nymph waited and waited for its friend the butterfly pupa to finish resting.

While the grasshopper nymph waited, it grew...

And grew... and grew...

When the grasshopper grew, it shed its old skin, or molted.

Finally, one day the grasshopper nymph noticed something different about its friend the butterfly pupa… the chrysalis seemed to be moving…

It was!

The butterfly pupa was awake and leaving its chrysalis!

The grasshopper nymph looked up and heard its friend say, "Look, grasshopper nymph! I am finally an adult; I am a butterfly! This is the final stage of my life cycle."

"Wow, butterfly! You look beautiful. I am sorry I did not believe you when we were eggs and you told me you would become a butterfly one day. You were telling the truth," said the grasshopper nymph.

"I must have been sleeping a long time. You have gotten much larger, grasshopper nymph!" exclaimed the butterfly. "Are you finished with your metamorphosis, too?"

"Not quite," the grasshopper replied and began to molt for the last time.

Under this last layer of skin, the grasshopper revealed newly formed wings.

"Look, butterfly, I have wings when I am an adult, too!" said the grasshopper.

"I am so happy that you stayed by me the whole time I was in my pupa stage," said the butterfly.

"That's what friends are for," said the grasshopper. "Friends are there for each other through…

ALL of life's stages!"

CPSIA information can be obtained
at www.ICGtesting.com
Printed in the USA
BVHW022216221121
622254BV00002B/30